This book belongs to:

....

....

Written by Ronne Randall

Illustrated by Estelle Corke

First published by Parragon in 2007

Parragon
Queen Street House
4 Queen Street
Bath BA1 1HE, UK

ISBN 978-1-4054-9428-1

Printed in China

Daddy's
Little
Boy

PaRRagon
Bath · New York · Singapore · Hong Kong · Cologne · Delhi · Melbourne

Tom and his daddy were best friends. They spent a lot of time together, and did so many things!

Tom helped Daddy in the garden and, every weekend,
he helped him wash the car.

Tom and Daddy played catch together,
and they played soccer in the park.

"That's my little boy!" Daddy would say proudly.

Daddy and Tom
even went to the
barbershop together.
"I want a haircut just
like Daddy's," Tom
told the barber.
"You're certainly
Daddy's little boy!" the
barber said.

Daddy decided to build a birdhouse for the back yard, and asked Tom to help him.

"You're a very good helper, Tom," Daddy said.

When the birdhouse was finished, Tom helped Daddy put it up in a big tree in the garden.

"I helped Daddy make that," he told his friend Jimmy,
who had come to play that afternoon.

One day, Daddy and Tom were looking at a book together. The book was about knights and castles. Tom looked at the pictures again and again.

"I wish I had a castle to play with," said Tom.
"I could have pretend battles!"
"Why don't we build a castle?" said Daddy.

"That's a great idea, Daddy!" said Tom. "I'll draw a picture of what it should look like."

He got some paper and his crayons, and drew a wonderful castle with turrets and a gatehouse, just like the one in the book.

"I'll use your picture to
make some plans,"
said Daddy.

When Daddy's plans were finished, he and Tom
went to buy the supplies they would need.

That afternoon, and all the next day, Tom and Daddy were busy at Daddy's workbench in the garage.

Daddy sawed the wood...

...and Tom helped him with the gluing and hammering.

Mommy looked at all the work Tom and Daddy had done.
"Well done, Tom," she said.
"You certainly are Daddy's little boy!"

At last, the castle was finished.

"It's fantastic, Daddy!"
exclaimed Tom.

"My little boy and I make a good
team!" said Daddy.

Daddy had a special surprise for Tom—some model knights to go with the castle!

"Thank you, Daddy!" said Tom, his eyes shining.

After dinner, Daddy and Tom had a pretend battle with the model knights. Tom's knights won!

That night, as Daddy tucked Tom into bed,
Tom said, "Daddy, am I still your little boy?"

"Of course you are," said Daddy.

"Although my knights can beat yours in a
battle?" asked Tom sleepily.

"Yes," said Daddy. "You will always be my
little boy."

"I'm glad," said Tom, and he fell
fast asleep.